For my lovely Mum. A.S.
To Mum, Dad, Chris, and Terry with love from the very privileged baby
of the family! L.M.

OXFORD
UNIVERSITY PRESS

Great Clarendon Street, Oxford OX2 6DP

Oxford University Press is a department of the University of Oxford.
It furthers the University's objective of excellence in research, scholarship,
and education by publishing worldwide in

Oxford New York

Auckland Cape Town Dar es Salaam Hong Kong Karachi
Kuala Lumpur Madrid Melbourne Mexico City Nairobi
New Delhi Shanghai Taipei Toronto

With offices in
Argentina Austria Brazil Chile Czech Republic France Greece
Guatemala Hungary Italy Japan Poland Portugal Singapore
South Korea Switzerland Thailand Turkey Ukraine Vietnam

Text copyright © Amber Stewart 2009
Illustrations copyright © Layn Marlow 2009

The moral rights of the author and artist have been asserted

Database right Oxford University Press (maker)

First published 2009

British Library Cataloguing in Publication Data available

ISBN: 978-0-19-272849-4 (hardback)
ISBN: 978-0-19-272850-0 (paperback)

10 9 8 7 6 5 4 3 2 1

Printed in China

Paper used in the production of this book is a natural,
recyclable product made from wood grown in sustainable forests.
The manufacturing process conforms to the environmental
regulations of the country of origin.

s bedtime for Button.

Amber Stewart & Layn Mar

Just Li Tonig

OXFO
UNIVERSITY

'My little bear cub must be tired,' said Mummy,
'after such a busy day.'
'Sweet dreams,' said Daddy.

As they kissed him goodnight,
Button thought sleepily about his day
and wondered what his dreams might bring.

He remembered lazing in the
early morning sunshine . . .

climbing with his
big sisters . . .

playing by their
favourite pool . . .

and finding
interesting insects,

even a ladybird with three spots on one wing and not
a single spot on the other. Button found it on the fallen
tree that looked like a big bear asleep in the grass.

Button had forgotten about the
big, scary tree-bear until that very moment.
Supposing it came into his dreams tonight?

He couldn't take the risk.

'Mummy! Daddy!' he called.

Button told them all about his scary tree-bear worry.

Daddy said, 'Shall I give you
something nice to think about
before you go to sleep?
Nice thoughts always keep
the bad ones away.'

'Yes please,' Button nodded,
feeling much braver about
the scary tree-bear already.

'Well,' wondered Daddy, 'shall I tell you about
a day when there were no scary things?
A day *so* happy that if you think of it tonight
only sweet dreams will come.'

'What day was that, Daddy?' asked Button.
Daddy kissed the top of his nose and said,
'The day you were born . . .'

'It was one of those days that started misty, but I knew
a hot and sunny day was just around the corner.'

'A bit like today?' asked Button.
'When I woke up I couldn't even
see over the berry bush!'

'Yes, just like today,' Daddy smiled, 'and on the day you were born, I gathered the juiciest berries and stickiest honey.'

'A bit like today?' asked Button,
as he remembered lying in the
warm sun eating his sweet
breakfast berries.

'Yes,' said Daddy, 'but even more delicious.'

'On the day you were born,'
Daddy continued, 'your big sisters were so
happy they found special presents for you . . .'

'Like my lucky pine-cone,' said Button,
'and my little log-boat! And did they want
to play with me too?'

'Oh yes!' laughed Daddy. 'They wanted to play
with you right there and then, but Mummy
said you needed to grow a little first . . .'

'And now I've grown!' said Button. 'We played so much today we had to jump in Two Rivers Pool to cool down.'

'When evening came,' remembered Daddy,
'I took you in my arms to watch your
first-ever sunset and sing you a lullaby.'

'Just like *every* evening,' yawned Button.
He loved watching the sun go down with Daddy
and singing songs that made them laugh.

'And on your very first night,' said Daddy quietly, 'you were so tired you fell fast asleep. Mummy and I watched over you, and no scary tree-bear or bad dreams came to disturb our little one.'

'Just like tonight?' said Button.
'Yes,' whispered Daddy.

And Daddy was right . . .
only sweet dreams came.